LADY GOLD INVESTIGATES
~ VOLUME 1

COMPANION SHORT STORIES TO GINGER GOLD MYSTERIES

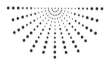

LEE STRAUSS

la plume PRESS

Library and Archives Canada Cataloguing in Publication Title: Lady Gold
investigates : a short read cozy historical 1920s mystery collection / Lee
Strauss. Names: Strauss, Lee (Novelist), author. Description: Short stories. |
Contents: v. 1. The Case of the Boy Who Vanished – The Case of the Missing
Fox Stole. Identifiers: Canadiana (print) 20190131608 | Canadiana (ebook)
20190131624 | ISBN 9781774090343 (v. 1 : softcover) | ISBN
9781774090350 (v. 1 : hardcover) | ISBN 9781774090336 (v. 1 : IngramSpark
softcover) | ISBN 9781774090312 (v. 1 : Kindle) | ISBN 9781774090329 (v. 1 :
EPUB) Classification: LCC PS8637.T739 L34 2019 | DDC C813/.6—dc23

THE CASE OF THE
VANISHING BOY

CHAPTER ONE

*T*he black and cream cradle telephone that sat on the counter of Ginger's Regent Street dress shop rang just as Ginger stepped inside. Madame Roux, her efficient shop manager, was busy with a customer—a tall, aristocratic-looking lady with a penchant for Schiaparelli.

She removed her gloves and placed them and her handbag behind the counter, then picked up the receiver and sang into it, "Good morning, Feathers and Flair. How may I help you?"

"Ginger?"

"Oliver!" She immediately recognised the voice of her friend Reverend, Oliver Hill.

"Yes. It's so good to hear your voice. I hope you're well."

"I'm doing quite well, thank you." Ginger was genuinely pleased to hear from the gentle vicar, though she was rather curious as to why he would seek her out at her shop. "I hope things are well with you too. Do tell me how things are at the church?"

One of the joys in Ginger's life was the Child Wellness Project that she had initiated with Oliver. The charity's main focus was feeding nutritious meals to street children twice a week, at the hall of St. George's Church.

"Everything is running as smoothly as can be expected. Numbers are up, and so are donations. We continue to have sufficient volunteers to help serve and cook the meals for the project, and lately there have even been some food donations from bakeries and grocers. I am quite encouraged."

"Oh, that is wonderful!"

"However, I have a concern that perhaps you can help with."

"Of course." Ginger retrieved a pencil and paper from under the counter. Finally, to the mystery behind Oliver's call.

"There is a young boy named Eddie, nine years old. I don't know his last name but he has been coming for meals for a quite a while now."

"The blond lad with the chipped front tooth?" Ginger asked. "Such an adorable youngster. I have had several amusing conversations with him. Boss just simply adores him. In fact they have become good friends." The child reminded her of Scout, her ward who had once lived on the streets. Scout was now a much-loved member of her household at Hartigan House, and though it had initially taken some adjustment for everyone, taking him in was something she had never come to regret. It was always inspiring to her how many of these young street children had such bright personalities and charm despite their sad circumstances in life. It broke Ginger's heart to see their innocence eroded much too early by the harshness of their existence.

"Yes, that's the one," Oliver replied. "Quite a bright young lad and very friendly. Some of the ladies who serve food are rather taken with him and have got to know him a little."

Ginger's heart pinched with worry. "Has something happened to Eddie?"

"It seems that he has gone missing."

"Oh mercy. Can you meet me right away at my office at Lady Gold Investigations? I want to give this my full attention until we find him again."

Oliver's answer was resolute. "I can be there in half an hour."

CHAPTER TWO

*G*inger walked from Feathers & Flair to the office around the corner on Watson Street and stepped inside, after first pausing outside the door to admire the new lettering: *Lady Gold Investigations.* The paint was barely dry and it seemed they might already have their first case.

Inside, the walls were papered with a beige and gold design, and there was a plush red rug on the wooden floor. The windows allowed in natural lighting and the whole place had a classy, yet business-like atmosphere. There were wine-coloured leather chairs there for clients to sit on that faced Ginger's walnut desk. There was also a small kitchen, a tastefully designed lavatory, and a dark room for developing photographs just down the corridor.

Felicia, Ginger's younger sister-in-law, had arrived earlier and had brought fresh scones from a bakery. When Ginger had first announced that she wanted to open an investigative office, Felicia had asked if she too could be part of the team. At first, Ginger had been slightly hesitant. She loved Felicia dearly, and since moving to London from Boston over a year before, they had become closer, almost as if they were real sisters. But she wasn't sure Felicia would be focused enough to be a part of an investigative team. Ginger's initial hesitancy had disappeared almost immediately when she observed how serious Felicia was, and the energy with which she threw herself into the work.

"Hello, Felicia. Oh, good," Ginger said referring to the scones. "Oliver shall be here presently. I'm afraid a waif is unaccounted for, and Oliver is concerned for his well-being. I've promised to help locate him."

Felicia's fingers paused over the tall keys of her black Remington typewriter—she wrote mystery stories when work at the office was slow—and got to her feet. "I'll make some tea."

Boss, Ginger's Boston terrier, whose small wicker bed was tucked behind Ginger's desk, popped his head up, alerted to the raised energy in the room. He stood and stretched out his back legs. Ginger reached down to give him a pat. She'd dropped him off earlier, before checking on matters at the dress shop, and he had obviously missed her in that short time.

Oliver arrived just as the kettle reached a boil. The bell above the door jangled and his lanky figure came through the small waiting area into the open office space. He was dressed in his usual black, casual trousers and shirt with the white dog collar. He carried a small leather briefcase and wore black shoes. His clerical garb contrasted with his slightly out-of-control carrot-coloured hair and his very fair skin. He was the only man Ginger knew who still had freckles despite being in his thirties. It gave him a certain boyish appearance that both Ginger and Felicia found very charming. Oliver and his wife, Matilda, were expecting a baby, and Ginger mused about what their child would look like. Would the babe be a redhead like its father, a trait Ginger shared, or dark like Matilda?

Ginger greeted Oliver with a warm handshake, then motioned to one of the leather chairs in front of her desk. "Please have a seat. Felicia's made tea."

"Oh, how do you do, Miss Gold?" Oliver said. "I hear you've been enjoying your new work here."

"I still help out at the dress shop when needed," Felicia replied. She carried the tea tray to Ginger's desk and distributed the saucers and teacups. "But I have more time to write whilst working here."

"Yes, that's right," Oliver said. "You're a published author now!"

Felicia flushed a little as she added milk to each cup, then poured the tea.

"Well, nothing's been published yet. Not until next year, they tell me."

"Publishing is notoriously slow," Ginger added.

Once they'd added sugar and settled in, Ginger turned the subject to the missing child.

"I'm afraid I don't have much money in the church treasury to pay for your troubles, Ginger, but I am hoping you might use your connections to make some enquiries for me on this matter."

"Oh, bish-bosh!" admonished Ginger. "I think you know me better than that! I shall spare no expense and give my full devotion to this until we discover the whereabouts of the boy. Neither you nor the church is going to spend one farthing paying any fee to me."

"My dear, I did suspect you would react this way," Oliver said with a smile. "But propriety dictates that I mention it anyway."

"Of course," Ginger replied. "Consider it mentioned."

"The boy has not shown up for any meals for several weeks now, which is highly unusual. The children that come for these meals almost always come back week after week. In addition, some of his closest mates have not seen him during that whole time," Oliver said. He removed a piece of sketch paper from his pocket, unfolded it, and laid it on the table. "This is a drawing of the boy."

"Why, that is amazing!" Felicia said. "Wherever did you get this?"

"One of the lads, a regular at the meals, is a very good artist, and he often sketches the other lads. He happened to do this sketch of Eddie the last time Eddie was at the church."

Both Ginger and Felicia stared at the drawing in astonishment.

"This really is a strikingly good resemblance," Ginger said. "It could be a big help. Composite drawings like this are often used by police these days to track down criminals or, as in this case, missing children. We should get a few copies made of this, Felicia. I believe there is a photostat office just around the corner from here."

Felicia collected the drawing. "I shall do."

"Tell us what you know of the boy's background, Oliver." Ginger said.

Oliver let out a long breath. "Well, I only know a little bit and details are scarce, but from what I can piece together from talking to the various children, it seems to be the typical story. He was born to an unwed mother who lived in various workhouses, which, as you know, even in our modern era are nothing more than harsh places where people are punished just for being poor. People who are all God's children, every one of them."

Oliver took a sip of his tea and then continued. "The system is set up for humiliation. Families are separated. The idea is that one should remove the children from their lazy parents—after all, why would you be poor unless you were lazy?"

Ginger was not used to hearing Oliver speak with such sarcasm. It was clear that he truly was bothered by the system.

"It's impossible to break the cycle of poverty," Oliver continued, "Ghastly idea, these workhouses. Any time spent in them as an adult is a stigma that clings to you forever."

He bent forward, putting sharp elbows on his bony knees. "Anyway, Eddie's mother grew ill and died when Eddie was just a nipper and the young lad, having no siblings at all, was able to somehow live on the streets by begging or stealing, as they do, or sometimes working and living at a workhouse. Apparently, he had some short stays in an orphanage, but they are constantly at capacity and many times children cannot stay there for long. Wintertime on the streets or even in a workhouse is especially desperate when it gets perishing cold. Eddie began showing up at St. George's for meals a few months ago, and quickly become a favourite among favourites, so to speak."

"Have you asked some of his chums if they know anything?" Felicia asked.

"Yes, we've all been asking. No one seems to know anything, or if they do, they're not talking. His mates all say that he simply disappeared from his usual haunts and street corners. It's very strange and it distresses me greatly."

Ginger waited for Oliver to take another drink of tea, giving him a chance to collect his emotions. Eddie's disappearance had affected her friend far more than he'd let on during their telephone call.

"Would you like a scone?" Felicia offered.

Oliver smiled weakly, then shook his head. "I've quite lost my appetite at the moment, but thank you."

"How about the possibility that some long-lost relatives of his mother have somehow learned about him and his whereabouts and have come to claim him?" Ginger asked.

"There is always that possibility," Oliver conceded, "but the chance seems to be very remote after all these years. Any relatives would have surely turned up years ago, I would think, when the news of the mother's death eventually reached them."

"There are a lot of places to look," Ginger said, endeavouring to sound hopeful. "Felicia and I can split up to double our efforts."

"Good idea," added Felicia.

Oliver stood and placed his hat back on his head. "In the meantime, I'll keep asking the children who come in to the meals and make sure copies of this sketch are posted prominently in our hall. It also won't hurt for us all to start praying in earnest, I think. There are so many nasty nooks and crannies in this massive city into which a little boy could disappear. Let's hope and pray the lad has not met with some skulduggery of some kind."

A small growl escaped Boss' lips.

The thought of nine-year-old Eddie alone on the streets of cold London, running into trouble with some low-minded, unscrupulous character, made Ginger's heart twist in her chest.

"God protect him," she said.

CHAPTER THREE

*G*inger rang the number of Scotland Yard and asked to speak to Chief Inspector Basil Reed.

"Oliver's been in to see me," she said, and then proceeded to explain the situation of the missing boy.

"Nasty business, Ginger," Basil added. "I'll do what I can to help, of course. But you do know that dozens of children go missing every day in our city, and while it's regrettable, I can't devote much of our already stretched resources to this in any official capacity."

"I suspected that already," Ginger said with a sigh, "but I would be grateful if you could check for me to see if any bodies that match Eddie's description have come to the police's attention in the last couple of weeks."

"Not that I know of, but I'll confirm it."

"Thank you, love."

"Since you have seen the boy and know his face, you could check with Dr. Gupta at the mortuary. Take a copy of your composite sketch with you to show him."

Ginger had already thought of this.

"Also, it would be good to bring several photostats to our

main office," Basil continued. "I think I can at least hang one on the main notice board here and send it to some of our other administrative locations. You never know if one of our constables has come across the boy."

"Thank you, Basil" Ginger said. "I'll send Felicia over when she has the photostat copies done."

"This one is close to your heart, isn't it, my dear?" Basil said in a gentle voice.

"Yes," she replied, her voice tinged with emotion. Basil knew how fond she was of Scout, and he'd begun to share her tender feelings for the boy.

"I have every confidence in you, of course," he said. "You are without a doubt the best person in all of London to be looking for this young lad."

Ginger hung up the telephone, dabbed her eyes with her handkerchief, and looked down at Boss, who was staring up at her from his basket. He emitted a low whimper and wagged his stumpy tail back and forth.

"C'mon, Boss," Ginger said. "There's no time for dilly-dallying now, is there?" She put on her hat and gloves. "Time to pay a visit to the good Dr. Gupta."

CHAPTER FOUR

*H*aving struggled through busy London traffic, Ginger and Boss finally arrived at the office of Dr. Manu Gupta at the London Medical School for Women. She parked the motorcar, then took a moment to admire the red brick building of the institution that had produced such notable women as pioneering geneticist Julia Bell and Doctor Florence Barret.

Ginger approached the building with some trepidation. She didn't relish the thought of discovering the body of the young boy here, nor would she welcome the task of delivering bad news to Oliver and the ladies who volunteered at the Child Wellness Project. She exhaled and straightened her shoulders before pulling open the door to the mortuary.

Dr. Manu Gupta, a striking Indian man in his mid-thirties, welcomed both her and Boss warmly, as was his custom.

"Always a pleasure," he said, "but usually the news you come with is not."

"I'm afraid you're correct in that assessment," Ginger replied. "I'm in search of a young boy, nine years old with blond hair. I do hope that you've not had anyone of that description come to you in the last couple of weeks?"

She removed a copy of the boy's sketch and handed it to the pathologist.

Dr. Gupta stared intently at the drawing for a long moment before saying, "To my memory there have not been any unidentified cadavers come into the mortuary that closely resemble this drawing. However, one can never be sure. The faces do take on a little bit of a different aspect in death, as you well know. We can go and take a look at the unidentified children's bodies that have come to us in the last few days. I think there are two in there now. That will rule out a few things at least."

Ginger decided to leave Boss for a few moments in Dr. Gupta's office whilst she and the doctor went to view the bodies. Boss seemed to particularly enjoy lying down on the pathologist's office chair, which made Dr. Gupta chuckle.

The bodies were kept in strict refrigeration, but Ginger knew that sometimes a cadaver could start to decompose if left waiting for identification too long. In addition, the smell of chemicals was sometimes very strong and she was sure Boss would appreciate being spared an assault of that type on his sensitive nose. One of the bodies turned out to be a young girl around the age of twelve. The other was a younger boy around eight, but he had strikingly dark hair— he was possibly of Indian descent like Dr. Gupta. There was no resemblance to the boy that Ginger had seen at St. George's.

"It's never a good day when we have to admit young children into our mortuary," Dr. Gupta said. "God rest their souls."

"Thank you for your time, Dr. Gupta," Ginger replied, happy to leave the corpses behind.

"Don't mention it. I shall be sure to keep an eye out, but let us keep hoping that your young friend never does come to my attention."

Ginger left the building a few minutes later with Boss tucked under her arm. She was glad to step out onto the street, inhale fresh air, and feel the sun on her face again.

"Well, that is one road that I am glad turned out to be a dead end," she said to Boss as she climbed back into her Crossley.

Instead of driving back to the office, Ginger decided to first drive to Hartigan House. Seeing those two dead children at the mortuary had made her suddenly want to see Scout, even though she had just seen him that morning. It was as if she wanted to hear the voice of a living child again. She also was interested to know if Scout had any ideas regarding the missing boy. Scout had lived on the streets of London for much of his eleven years and might have some insights that were not obvious to Ginger or the other adults involved in this search.

Ginger found her ward in the stable giving her Akhal-Teke gelding, Goldmine, a brushing.

"I've already done up Sir Blackwell," he said with a toothy grin, nodding his head in the direction of Basil's Arabian. "Just finishing up 'ere."

"Take your time," Ginger replied. "We can talk whilst you work. I only had a question about a street lad who's gone missing."

Scout's cap poked out from around Goldmine's neck. "Who's 'at?"

"A lad called Eddie. A little younger than you, with blond hair. Has a chipped front tooth."

Scout shrugged. "Can't say I know 'im."

"Do you think a boy like Eddie might have just wandered off to another area of London and established himself in another place, so to speak?" Ginger asked. "I mean, I don't think we really would have any way of knowing if he did decide to do that. Maybe he had a falling out with one of the young lads at the mealtimes at St. George's and decided to move on."

"That would be 'ard to believe, missus. Getting a good meal reg'lar and 'aving good mates to watch yer back is sometimes the difference between makin' it or not. We rely on each uvva. All of us had one fing in common: we were always 'ungry." The lad stared down at his feet as if ashamed for a moment, then looked up at Ginger. "The folks at St. George's is kind to the street kids. I fink a smart bloke like Eddie would know not to run off to try to find sumfin' else."

"That's what I thought too," Ginger added.

"I know the workhouse he was at sometimes, the workhouse at Dowgate. It's not far from St. George's. I 'eard it's a decent place as far as those sorts of places go. Terrible food and thin soup, but a lad could live on it. Maybe 'e's back there."

Ginger made a mental note to get Felicia to visit Dowgate Workhouse.

"If there's any way I can 'elp, just let me know," said the boy sincerely.

Ginger gave her ward a pat on the back. "Thank you, Scout. I have to leave again, but I'll be back for supper. You'll join us again, so be sure to clean up."

"Yes, missus."

Ginger smiled and raised a brow. Scout was officially her ward, but she was intent on making him more than that. In her heart, Scout was already her son.

At Ginger's look, Scout corrected himself. "Yes, Mum."

Ginger and Boss climbed into the Crossley. She had a bit of a drive ahead of her to Hanwell, which was situated on the outskirts of London. It was time to start digging a little deeper.

CHAPTER FIVE

*G*inger, with Boss right behind her, stepped out of the Crossley directly in front of the huge red brick building known as the Hanwell Residential Industrial School. The school was well known to most Londoners, but Ginger had mixed feelings towards it. It was an imposing structure with adjoining wings for children's dormitories, superintendent offices, medical wings, several sports halls, classrooms, and workshops for training. Altogether, the school could accommodate eight hundred students. Children, chosen from among the poorest, were sent here by the authorities from all over the city. They were trained for industry with programmes for literacy, carpentry, and much more. A strong emphasis was placed on moral discipline and the school had a reputation for harsh treatment, especially for boys. Ginger knew this, but also knew that there were far worse places a boy could end up. Unlike the mortuary, Ginger harboured some hope that Eddie had somehow come here, perhaps having been randomly picked up near St. George's Church by one of the school's admittance officers.

After asking for directions at the main reception, Ginger

made her way to the northeast corner of the site, to a T-shaped administration building where children were housed on arrival at the school. She passed several large classrooms and one large and noisy workshop where children seemed to be engaged in building wooden furniture. The smell of teak oil and sawdust was suddenly in the air which, of course, made Boss sneeze as he trotted resolutely beside Ginger, his little claws clicking away on the tiled floor. Ginger was somewhat pleased to see that the children she observed had clean and decent uniforms and, in contrast to the gaunt faces at St. Georges, a certain childhood chubbiness to their faces. This was a good sign. The general atmosphere was one of earnestness and focus.

A rather dour-looking woman in a dreary slate-blue frock, who sat behind the counter of the admittance station, examined the sketch. "I can think of one boy that has come here recently that could match this drawing." Ginger's heart skipped a beat. Perhaps the search was going to end with positive news. The woman shot Boss a disapproving look that made Ginger fear a reprimand was coming, but she merely continued. "He was admitted under the name of Theodore Smith. As is the case for a lot of children we have here, a family name is sometimes hard to come by. They often just make one up and we have neither the means, nor the time to search for birth records. So the last name could be suspect. However, 'Theodore' could be a long form for Eddie, I suppose. Theodore was admitted three weeks ago."

"Is there any way I could meet him now?" asked Ginger hopefully.

"The schedule I have here shows that he is at the moment doing exercise. If you exit this building at the rear and walk across the courtyard, you'll come to a sports field. You should spot him from the sideline. Just ask the games master to point him out to you."

It took a few moments for Ginger to find the sports field. She then headed for a middle-aged man who stood on the side of it. He was very tall, about six feet four inches, was dressed in grey tweed trousers and waistcoat and black leather cleated football shoes. A flat cap rested on his mass of curly hair, and around his neck he wore a whistle that appeared to be well used. He was apparently enjoying shouting instructions to a group of young boys engaged in a game of football on a grass field. It seemed to Ginger that the lads had not much organisation on the field and were running pell-mell after the ball. Boss barked once, which was rare. Ginger had to actually hold him back on the leash slightly.

"I'm sure they would appreciate you entering the game, Boss," she said with a chuckle. "But your renown as a footballer has probably not reached this field yet."

Ginger scanned the field as she approached the tall man, but could not see any sign of Eddie. Perhaps he was on an adjacent field. "Excuse me. My name is Mrs. Reed, and I represent Lady Gold Investigations." With a surprised look, the man turned his attention from the boys to Ginger.

"Bloomin' 'eck. A lady private investigator? One o' my lads must've done somefin' this time." He let out a low whistle. "Weatherby's my name." Mr. Weatherby crouched down low to give Boss a pat and rough shake on the head with both hands. "And 'ow are you, me 'ole mucker, eh?" Boss wagged his tail stub furiously and licked the man's hand.

"None of your lads are in trouble as far as I know," Ginger said, as the man rose back to his full height. "I'm simply looking for a child who may have gone missing. I'm told that

21

you have a young lad named Theodore on your field this morning."

"Yes, he came in a few weeks ago by one of our admittance officers. He was all on 'is own all right. Not much of a footballer, 'e is. But that'll change." He pointed to the goalkeeper on one of the teams. "There 'e is, in goal today as you can see."

Ginger's heart sank as soon as she saw the boy. It was obvious the lad was much heavier and taller than the missing boy, and didn't resemble the sketch Oliver had given her at all.

Eddie wasn't here.

CHAPTER SIX

The next morning at the office of Lady Gold Investigations, Ginger and Felicia sat down to compare notes.

"If I don't see the inside of another taxi for a while, it will be alright with me," Felicia said. "I've already checked with every workhouse within a ten-mile radius of St. George's Church. Five in all. It was a rather depressing and very full day. That's why I didn't make it back to Hartigan House until the evening. Some of those places are simply ghastly. I've never encountered so many sad faces all in one day." Felicia took a bite of a fresh scone and dusted the crumbs from her chin. "I showed the picture to the main officer at each one of them. They were quite helpful for the most part. None of the boys I saw even came close to the sketch, though there were several that went by the name of Eddie."

"Oh dear." Ginger sank deeper into her chair.

"However," Felicia continued after a sip of tea, "at one of the last workhouses I visited, the Lion's Head Union Work-house, the warden gave me an interesting tip."

"What's that?" Ginger asked, looking up from the sketch

of their Eddie she was absentmindedly looking at for the hundredth time.

"He told me that there is a rumour about the master of a workhouse south of London in Croydon. Apparently, he runs a small workhouse that is not officially connected with the authorities or with the local parish."

"Why would he do that?"

"Most workhouses, as deplorable as they are, still have to abide by certain minimal laws such as length of working day and severity of punishments. That is outlined in *The Poor Law Amendments.*" Felicia had a twinkle in her eye and she nodded slightly, as if Ginger should be impressed by her research.

"Most workers are engaged in industries such as shoe-making, tailoring, and even crushing bones for fertiliser," Felicia continued. "Furthermore, many workhouses exchange lodging for several hours' work each day. Workers are not prisoners and children are not allowed to be kept working past a certain time. The rumour is that this partic-ular workhouse master not only has a disregard for any of these rules, resulting in even more deplorable working conditions, he also keeps the children captive, and they are not allowed to leave at any time. In effect, making it a prison."

"How shocking!" gasped Ginger, her eyes wide open.

"He 'employs' children only, since they eat less food and are more easily controlled by force," Felicia added. "The person I talked to at Lions Head told me that there is also suspicion that the workhouse, ironically called 'Fool's End Workhouse', is a front for organised illegal addictive drug trade."

"What makes you think Eddie has ended up in such an out-of-the-way, hellish place?" Ginger asked.

"Two reasons. Number one is that the master of this

workhouse, a Mr. Crealy, apparently has the practice of driving around parts of London in a lorry and luring children with the promise of food and then simply kidnapping them in broad daylight."

"This story just keeps getting worse," Ginger said in amazement. "And number two?"

"I drove to Fool's End as my last stop of the day." Felicia leaned in with a look of earnestness. "I think I saw him. I think our little Eddie is there."

A thrill of excitement bubbled in Ginger's chest. "How sure are you?"

"Unfortunately I can't be certain." Felicia let out a small huff. "Crealy wouldn't allow me past the admittance office. He seemed friendly enough at the outset, but when I pulled out the sketch he suddenly grew hostile. No manners at all, that one. I had a mind to give him some words of my own."

"Well, then how did you see the boy?"

"On my way out, as I was going through a small courtyard, I looked up at a second-storey window and I saw a boy standing there looking out. My view of him was fairly clear. Although I have never met him, to me he looked just like this Eddie." Felicia tapped the sketch with a long painted fingernail. "I waved at him and he waved back. He looked a very sad, poor lad. Then someone came and pulled him away from the window."

Ginger sat up straight. "I am going in there."

"Are you going to take Basil?" Felicia asked, unmasked concern in her eyes.

"I don't think it would do any good. Until I can prove that a crime has been committed, Basil wouldn't get any further than you did. One has to have a reason to approach a judge for a warrant to search a place of business. One must almost catch them red-handed. No, taking Basil in there at this point will only threaten Crealy and God knows then what might happen to little Eddie."

"What on earth do you plan to do?" Felicia asked, "If I didn't make it very far, and even Basil cannot take a step further, then what?"

Ginger held up a palm, stopping Felicia short. "Mr. Crealy is about to get another unexpected visit. I believe a change in tactics is in order." Ginger pushed away from her desk and rose to her feet. "Come along, Felicia, we're going to shop for some clothing in a way that you have never done before."

CHAPTER SEVEN

*O*riginally starting out as the Salvation Army's 'salvage brigade' in 1897, the idea of salvaging and re-using clothing had started to catch on as more and more people flooded into the city. After the war, shops had started to sprout up to sell used clothing that still had some wear left in them. Ginger understood that these types of shops were a godsend to many people who simply could not afford new clothes for their children or for themselves. She predicted that soon there would be many more shops like this one across England. William Booth had died a short while ago, in 1912, but his charitable legacy lived on.

"They are going to think we are lost," Felicia said. "And I would tend to agree."

The building, which was a narrow shop sandwiched between a French café and a tailor's shop, had a small window display. There were several wickerwork mannequins set up that were wearing various forms of garb. Felicia stopped on the pavement to look at one of them that had been dressed in a blue cotton frock with a springtime floral design and a straw hat which boasted an extravagant white feather.

"Oh, this one isn't bad," Felicia remarked.

Ginger laughed. "You can try it on."

"Not on your life!" Felicia exclaimed. "Someone's already worn that. No telling who, either."

"I want t' find a new 'at," Scout chimed in. Ginger and Felicia had called into Hartigan House to collect the boy, who was more than happy to have a part to play in rescuing young Eddie. "I'll bet they 'ave one my size."

"Go ahead and look," Ginger said, "You might find one to your liking."

"Thanks, Mum!"

As they entered the shop, two of the lady attendants working at the counter immediately looked up in surprise. The younger woman said, "Why, Lady Gold! I never expected to see you in this shop." About the same age as Felicia, she was pleasant looking with very kind, smiling eyes.

Ginger was not embarrassed, but she was surprised. "Have we met?"

"I'm dreadfully sorry, where are my manners? We have not been introduced, but I have seen you before in your wonderful boutique shop. Last time I was there I bought a lovely French hat. Such a hat is not easy to find and I have worn it twice already to social engagements we have hosted at our manor. I'm Miss Littleton." She offered her hand.

"So very pleased to meet you," Ginger said, politely shaking hands. "I go by Mrs. Reed now, generally."

"Oh, yes, you married. I read about it in the society pages." She paused, glancing at her feet shyly. "I suppose you're wondering what I'm doing in a place like this?"

With a smile, Ginger encouraged her to continue.

"I'm a volunteer. I try to come in a couple of times a

week." Then, as if to answer the unspoken question hanging in the air, she added, "It gives me satisfaction to know that I am helping in a small way. My family are Methodists and have close ties to General William Booth and his efforts." She paused. "And what, may I ask, is of interest to you today here at our humble little shop?" She smiled broadly as she took in Felicia and Scout in one glance.

Ginger noticed that Felicia looked a bit nervous, as if she had been caught doing something naughty, or perhaps she just hadn't expected to meet one of her peers.

"A costume," Ginger said, "We need to find something my size that would make me look like I was, well, from a rather more humble background."

"Oh, what fun!" Miss Littleton exclaimed. She looked like she was about to ask the reason why Ginger would want to do such a thing, but Scout chimed in.

"An' I'm lookin' for an 'at!"

Miss Littleton shot a questioning glance at Ginger, but propriety forbade her to ask about Ginger's connection to the lad. "Oh, I am a certain we have something for a handsome young man like you!" At this, Scout's face immediately turned a bright red. Even his ears had gone suddenly crimson! Ginger held in a smirk. Her charge was reacting to the attractive young lady who'd called him handsome.

Ginger cast a warning glance at Felicia, who looked like she might burst out laughing.

While Miss Littleton was assisting Scout in his quest for a hat, Ginger and Felicia took a look around. The clothes were arranged in neat rows according to size and description. Dresses were arranged on hanger racks as were men's waistcoats and jackets. Ginger was surprised at the condition of some of the items. They looked almost brand-new.

"Well, let's start from the feet up, shall we?" Ginger said.

An hour later they all exited the shop. Ginger carried several different outfits, including two pairs of leather shoes that Felicia had found that looked like they had walked to Scotland and back, originally made from thick leather for durability. Ginger had also acquired a couple of bonnets, as she knew that most women of the working class did not wear hats, but favoured bonnets to keep the hair off the face and away from factory machinery. The frocks she had purchased were typical working women's wear, one made of dark cotton and the other of wool, to hide the dirt. Scout had found a smart-looking cap that looked almost new, albeit a bit too big. Ginger assured him that one day soon it would fit perfectly as he grew. He also carried an outfit for himself that was worn and patched.

Not to forget Boss, who'd slept through the shopping experience while waiting in the motorcar, Ginger had found a faded red scarf. When she tied it around his neck, he looked formally dressed and ready for some grand canine occasion. He and Scout were quite a pair, sitting tall in the backseat.

"Well, I am glad that's over," Felicia said as she gathered her skirt and closed the door to the passenger seat. Ginger cringed inwardly. Felicia still had a lot to learn about not taking privilege for granted and that some things transcend social class.

"There but for the grace of God go I," she said.

Felicia stared back with wide eyes. "I beg your pardon?"

"It's a quote from John Bradford," Ginger explained as she started the engine. "He meant to say that good people recognise that we are all God's children, and that social standing is temporal. In the end it is meaningless."

Felicia said nothing as they rumbled away.

CHAPTER EIGHT

*W*hen Ginger emerged from the fitting room at Feathers & Flair, Felicia couldn't hold in her astonishment. "Oh my goodness!" It was after hours in the late afternoon and the shop was empty. "That is a transformation."

Ginger had tied her bright red hair underneath the bonnet, except for a few loose strands which hung down on her face, and she had scrubbed all her makeup off her face. The dark brown cotton frock had a large, faded white collar and an embroidered belt around the middle which was stained. The hem reached down to her ankles, and though the frock was clean, it had a slightly stale smell. Obviously too large, Ginger had chosen it for the purpose of stuffing in a pillow that she had borrowed from her seamstress, Emma, who used it to support her back while she sewed.

Ginger regarded her profile in the full-length mirror. Could she pass for a woman with child and close to her due date?

This will work, she thought to herself. It wasn't the first time Ginger had played the part of a poorer woman, and she felt a rush of memories come back to her as she gazed at the image in the mirror. She recognised that lady staring back at her. Her experiences as a spy in the Great War had once again equipped her for tasks in the present day that no one, not even her husband, could imagine her capable of. British Intelligence had forbidden all former spies to divulge their activities, even after the war. It was a part of her life that held both good and bad memories for her. Both kinds brought her deep emotion when she recalled them in her quiet moments.

Casting those thoughts aside, she asked, "What do you think?"

"I hardly recognise you," Felicia said.

"Me neither," Scout added. His little face pinched with emotion. "I don't think I like you like this, Mum."

"It's just pretend, love," Ginger said. "For a good cause."

Boss barked approvingly at Ginger's feet, and Ginger tried but failed to bend over to pat him.

"Oof! This tummy really is a nuisance."

"One more thing." Ginger walked over to the iron coal-burning stove at the back of the building that kept the shop heated in the winter months, reached down into the cold grate, and brought up a small handful of ashes which she lightly spread on her cheek and the front of her skirt. She also rubbed some on Boss' back, right side, and the top of his head where he couldn't lick it off. "Sorry, me ol' mucker," Ginger said in a perfect Cockney accent. "I 'ave the notion that you an' me 'ave an appointment wiv a certain scallywag an' I need ya to be lookin' ready for th' part."

Ginger would have loved to have had her camera at the ready at that moment to snap a picture of the expression on Felicia's and Scout's faces.

.   .   .

FOOL'S END Workhouse was situated in a very run-down area of East Croydon, not far from the train station. It was a simple three-storey brick pavilion-style building, with a central tower in the middle that looked dirty and in need of a coat of paint on the doors and windows. The main entrance was a squeaky door on the ground floor of the tower. Ginger, Felicia, and Scout, along with Boss, had arrived in the motorcar and had parked a couple of streets away next to a red and white K1 telephone kiosk. The Crossley didn't match the neighbourhood, nor their current style of dress, and it needed to be kept out of sight.

"Give us thirty minutes," Ginger said, as she quieted the engine. "If we don't return, use that public telephone to ring Basil."

Felicia pointed to her wristwatch. "Be careful!"

Ginger and Scout, with Boss tagging along, approached the workhouse on foot, looking like they had just spent the last week living on the street. The ragged trio entered the reception area which contained a small wooden desk and chair with a phone. The place had a dusty smell and Ginger could see that no one had swept even the office area for quite some time. The windows had bars and there were padlocks on most of the doors leading away from the reception to the interior of the building.

The station appeared to be untended.

"'ello," Ginger called. "Anyone 'ere?"

The sound of heavy machinery could be heard coming from somewhere in the building as well as the sound of hammers striking stone and metal.

They walked past the reception area and down a corridor that looked like it led to a larger hall. The place had the ambience of a prison.

Suddenly, out of a double doorway came a gruff-looking

middle-aged man. Heavy-set with greasy, thinning hair, he was dressed in a grey woollen shirt and waistcoat that were stained with grease, as though he had just been up to his elbows in fixing machinery. The same grease had dirtied the lines of his hands.

"'ere now. An' oo are you?" he said in an irritated voice. He pivoted on a worn-out shoe to quickly lock the door behind him with a padlock key. Ginger wondered why he felt the need to lock it.

"Forgive me, sir," Ginger said. She made a show of holding her belly as if the child within was causing discomfort, but she also wanted to make sure the pillow didn't dislodge.

"My name is Sally Green, an' this 'ere is my nephew Billy. We's bin wonderin' about this 'ere establishment. Billy 'ere is a very 'ard worker an' things been very difficult fer us in the last while since 'is dad run off an' 'is mum died. I can't afford the time to tend to 'im no more, an' you can see that soon I'll 'ave another mouf t' feed. My own 'usband is gone now. The bottle took 'im is th' sad truth. In any case, I was 'opin' ta meet the master 'ere."

"That's me. I'm Mr. Crealy." The stern man looked down suspiciously at Boss. He came a few steps closer to get a better look at Scout and then smiled. For some reason this made Ginger shudder with disgust. Scout immediately took off his cap and said, "'Ow d'ya do, sir?"

"Well I do just fine," Crealy replied. He looked at Ginger. "We can always use a good worker. I'm not in the 'abit of takin' in children who still got family around, and at the moment we got no room fer you 'ere."

"Well, I'm 'opin' to get a job o' work at the fact'ry after I 'ave my babe, so you won't see me 'round much." Ginger knew that Crealy would be reluctant to agree to take a child that had someone who might check on him from time to time, which was why she'd spun the yarn about being an aunt who had been suddenly saddled with a distant nephew, and about to have her own baby. That situation would pose less of a threat.

"Well, I s'pose we could consider the boy," Crealy said. After a pause, he added, "'ere, let's go into my office and see if there's an empty spot for 'im. Can you leave 'im 'ere now?"

"We'd 'ave to go an' get Billy's belongin's," Ginger said. "He has a few more trousers and that but we could be back later in the day." Of course, Ginger had no intention of leaving Scout there at all.

"That would aw'right, I s'pose," Crealy said, "But the lad would be fine to stay while you collected his things."

"Thank you, sir, but I promised 'im 'e could say 'is farewells."

Mr. Crealy let out a disgruntled sigh, "As you wish."

"I was wonderin' if I could just 'ave a look inside to see where Billy would be workin' or maybe just a look at the eatin' 'all or somethin'?" Ginger was hoping that Crealy would be willing to show at least a small part of the building so she could get a sense of where things were. Perhaps she would see something that she could alert the authorities about, or possibly even catch a sight of Eddie. It was a bit of a gamble but Ginger was determined. "Just to appease me own nerves."

"Now, you listen 'ere, miss—"

"It'll only take a minute."

"Oh, blast it anyway. I don't want to disturb the work 'ere but maybe a quick look into the refectory would be in order. I can tell ya that all the workers are 'ealthy and 'appy 'ere. They get good, regular grub 'ere and a bath ev'ry week."

He led them down the hall and unlocked the large double,

swinging doors that led directly into a large hall with stone floors. There were long rows of wooden tables and benches with enough seating for around one hundred and fifty people. On the side were open doors that revealed a large open kitchen, which at the moment was completely empty. On the far end of the hall was another open double door that exposed a short corridor that ended in a *T*.

"There's nothin' but good food served 'ere," Crealy began. He looked uncomfortable as if he were trying to distract Ginger from looking down the hallway.

It was time for Ginger to make her move.

Crying out, she doubled over and grabbed her midsection. "Ohh! Oh dear!" Scout, who'd stayed close behind her, put a hand on her back as if to steady her.

Crealy looked worried. "'Old on now!"

"I'll be aw'right, th' baby ain't due for 'nother two weeks," Ginger said. "Maybe I can just sit down somewhere." Crealy and Scout helped her to a bench where she sat down, blowing air out of her cheeks as if in immense pain. She'd never given birth herself, but she'd witnessed the miracle on more than one occasion.

"The baby's not comin' now is it?" Scout said, practically shouting. "The pains 'aven't come afore now!"

At this revelation Crealy blanched.

"Oh, I 'ope not, Billy," Ginger wheezed. She suddenly let out another long "Oooohh."

"Do ya need some water? Mebbe I'll go and fetch the missus." Mr. Crealy's nose wrinkled at being put out in such a manner.

"Oh, I 'ate to be a bother, but per'aps that's a good idea," Ginger said, grimacing for good measure. "Oooh dear. Oh my goodness!"

Mr. Crealy ran off like a bolt of lightning.

CHAPTER NINE

*A*t that instant Boss suddenly let out a small yelp and bolted down the opposite corridor. Boss hadn't run from Ginger since he was a puppy and she was shocked at the dog's sudden behaviour.

"Boss, come back here!"

Ginger and Scout shared a stunned look, and then started running after the dog, an effort not made easy for Ginger by the pillow stuffed in her frock. Boss headed down the empty corridor, turned right, and barked once more. Out of several doorways on either side peeked small children dressed in work clothes, to watch the unusual sight of a small black and white dog running away from a lady obviously with child and her lad, but some adults in tattered staff uniforms reached out a hand and yanked the children back into the rooms.

Suddenly Boss, Ginger, and Scout burst through another set of swinging doors that opened to a large outer courtyard filled with emaciated children. At the far end of the walled space was a huge pile of rocks and on the left was a large mechanised sifting machine. The children, all dressed in tattered clothing, were engaged in breaking and sorting rocks. One might have presumed the stones were to be used in road building, but in any case, it was back-breaking work. Ginger and Scout caught a glimpse of Boss at the very far end of the yard leaping into the lap of a thin and very dirty blond-haired child. The lad sat on a small bench as he chipped rocks against a large steel anvil with a hammer. He dropped his hammer to hug the dog, a look of sheer disbelief on his face. "B…B…Boss? Is that you?"

Ginger and Scout ran over to the lad. He had lost considerable weight since Ginger had seen him last, and his clothes were rags hanging on his small frame. He had a large bruise on the left side of his face around his eye, which was half closed from the swelling.

"Eddie!" Ginger cried once she had caught her breath.

"Lady Gold? Is that you?"

He dropped Boss to the ground as he regarded her clothes and her stomach in bewilderment.

"Shh," Ginger whispered. "We're here to get you out of this place."

At the sight of the boy's condition, Ginger's heart turned over in her chest. This workhouse needed to be shut down!

Boss suddenly turned and growled in the direction of the other side of the yard.

"'Ang on, then!" Crealy stood at the door with a miserable-looking middle-aged woman. Her small eyes were filled with anger, and she carried a stick of some kind that Ginger was sure was used for beating. They were accompanied by two men dressed in tattered staff uniforms who slowly started towards Ginger and the two boys. Ginger was aware of the vulnerability of her situation but she did not let herself feel intimidated. Instead she rose up straight.

"Wot's 'appened to the baby pains then?" Mrs. Crealy asked.

"This lad is Billy's brother and me other nephew," Ginger said, "We've been wonderin' where 'e got off to." She grabbed Eddie's hand, ignoring the question.

"Where d'ya fink yer goin' wif 'im?" Crealy said.

"I've changed my mind. I'm not sure I like the looks of this place. I think I've a mind t' take these boys 'ome wiv me, such as it is," Ginger said.

Mr. and Mrs. Crealy stared at each other. Ginger knew that this was a very complex situation here for them. They couldn't very well stop an expectant woman from leaving, but if they forced her to leave Eddie here, she would no doubt report them to the police, and they'd be charged with forced confinement.

Ginger did not wait for a response. "C'mon, lads."

She walked the boys past the stunned guards who looked questioningly at the Crealys for some kind of instruction. Mr. and Mrs. Crealy stood there looking enraged and confused at what to do next. Ginger was hoping that they would come to the conclusion that if they just let her and the boys leave, there would be no reason to go to the authorities.

Ginger led the way out through the corridor from which they had emerged and headed for the exit. The Crealys followed a menacing distance behind. To Ginger's dismay, someone had locked the door with a padlock. She stopped and stared at Mr. Crealy with a look of impatience.

Crealy, with a contemptuous frown on his face, unlocked and swung open the door to the pavement outside. The boys, with Boss in tow, walked out into the low light of dusk. Just as Ginger thought they were home free, Crealy stepped in front of her and braced his arm against the doorjamb to stop her exit.

"I don't know oo you think you are, comin' 'ere and takin' one of my lads. I don't appreciate the likes of you at all and if I ever see either you or yer nephews around 'ere again..." He let that hang in the air. "An' don't ever come beggin' around 'ere for work or to drop off yer bastard child." He grimaced as he pointed towards Ginger's belly.

Ginger looked him straight in the eye. "I have dealt with much more dangerous thugs than you in my time, Mr. Crealy. Your threats do not frighten me in the least. But I am warning you now that you will not like what will happen to this workhouse next."

At the obvious change in her accent, Crealy's face went white.

"Remove your arm at once!" Ginger commanded.

Crealy, cowed, dropped his arm and stepped aside. Ginger joined the boys and Boss as they hurried away.

"'ere now!" Crealy shouted after them, his voice slightly wavering. "What d'ya mean by that?"

CHAPTER TEN

A few weeks later, Ginger poked her head into the woodworking training class at Hanwell Industrial Residential School.

"Boss!"

A boy's voice cried out in surprise. Eddie dropped his wood chisel beside a small, partially completed chair that he and another lad were working on. He ran over and bent down to hug the Boston terrier while getting licked liberally all over his small face by the exuberant dog. The other children in the class stopped what they were doing to watch in surprise. It was not every day they saw a dog in their classroom.

"Well, hello to you too," Ginger said. She watched the happy scene with a smile.

Ginger was pleased to see that in the last little while Eddie had gained back some of the weight he had lost and that the bruises on his face were almost gone. He seemed clean and healthy and was wearing a new school uniform.

"Good morning, Mrs. Reed." The instructor for the class walked over to shake her gloved hand. He was a balding man dressed in a carpenter's work clothes and smelled of sawdust. "I was told to expect you today."

"Good morning, Mr. Browning," Ginger returned. She nodded at Eddie. "How is he doing?"

"The young lad's coming along just fine. He seems to be well liked here, both by the staff and the other children."

"I'm not surprised," Ginger said. Young Eddie was a delight.

"He's a bright, well-behaved young lad, I am happy to say. A good addition to our school." Mr. Browning peered down at Eddie, who was on his knees stroking Boss on the back.

Ginger knew that it was not an easy life at Hanwell School. The rules were strictly enforced and the administration had a reputation for expecting a lot from the children in terms of learning and obedience. However, intuitive children who could adjust to the austere life here usually did well and left with a chosen skill that could earn them a satisfactory wage as a tailor, plumber, carpenter, or one of a myriad of other trades. The children who ended up in Hanwell and stayed there were much better off than the ones who were forced to spend their younger years in workhouses, or worse, on the streets of London fending for themselves.

"Would you mind if I spoke to Eddie for a few minutes?" Ginger asked

"Of course not." Mr. Browning checked a scratched pocket watch. "His next lesson, which is arithmetic, is in twenty-five minutes time. Please bring him back here before then, if you will."

Ginger and Eddie, with Boss, strolled to a small outside courtyard. It was a sunny spring day and Ginger enjoyed the sound of the birds flying overhead. They chose a bench and Boss sat at Ginger's feet.

"Eddie," Ginger began gently, "I want to hear from you

directly how things are going. You never have to keep anything from me. If you are ever having some kind of difficulty here I want to know about it. All right?"

Eddie nodded solemnly, "Things are aw'right 'ere. I've 'ad to get my 'ead on straight and mind me p's and q's, if you know what I mean. But I am enjoyin' learnin' how to work the wood. There's even a swimmin' pool 'ere. I'm learning 'ow ta swim!"

"Splendid!"

"The food 'ere ain't as good as at St. George's though, but it's aw'right 'nuff." He paused for a moment, looking at the ground. "I already 'ave some good mates 'ere but I do miss everyone there at the church."

"I have arranged for you to visit twice a month to have some evening meals," Ginger said. "Scout and I shall pick you up to take you. It's all been arranged, so long as it doesn't interfere with your studies here and you maintain your current good behaviour."

"Blimey, that'd be just fine… just fine wiv me!"

Eddie flushed with excitement, then paused for a moment, deep in thought. Finally, in a very serious, small voice that made Ginger's heart go out to the young lad, he said, "I 'ate t' think ol' Mr. Crealy is still out there snatchin' children off the street like he did with me."

What a terrible thing for any child to go through! Ginger put her arm around him.

"Rest assured, Mr. Crealy will be doing no such thing any longer. I immediately reported what I saw, along with some of the awful things you told me, to my husband at Scotland Yard. He's a chief inspector there, did you know?"

Eddie looked up, surprised.

Ginger continued, hoping the child would understand. "There was enough evidence there for him to send in a team of investigators, who arrived unannounced at the workhouse two days after I came for you. They closed the place down for good."

Ginger had shortened the tale on Eddie's account. The investigating officers had found that not only were the Crealys unlawfully confining and mistreating children, they were also using part of the building as storage for a criminal gang in London that dealt with illegal drugs. The Crealys had both been remanded in custody and were awaiting trial. The children they had imprisoned had been placed in better situations, some of them here at Hanwell.

"Crikey!" Eddie said. A moment later he grinned up at her and said, "After seeing 'ow you 'andled ol' Crealy, I wouldn't want t' get on your bad side, Mrs. Reed!"

At this, Ginger chuckled and tousled Eddie's mess of blond hair.

"By the way, 'ow's the new baby comin' along?" He guffawed, pointing at her belly.

At this Ginger laughed out loud. No wonder the boy was such a favourite. "You are going to do just fine in this world, Eddie."

They said their goodbyes, and Ginger carried Boss across the street to the Crossley. "You were the hero of the day back at that awful workhouse, Bossy."

Boss barked once as he leaped onto the front seat.

"I think I may have a dog treat waiting for you back at Hartigan House."

THE END

THE CASE OF THE MISSING
FOX STOLE

CHAPTER ONE

*M*rs. Ginger Reed had just tidied away the remaining pressing matters of the day at the office of Lady Gold Investigations when she received a phone call from Emma Miller, the seamstress and resident dress designer who worked in her boutique fashion shop, Feathers & Flair.

"I'm working on a design right now that I am bit stuck on," Emma said, "and I wondered if you might have some ideas. I really love this one and I think it's going to be a popular dress design, but I would value your opinion before I go much further."

"How exciting!" Ginger said. "Yes, I'll be over shortly." Ginger had the feeling that Emma would one day become a very important designer in the world of high fashion, at least in London. Indeed, since Ginger had opened the dress shop, the young woman's talents had become the talk of the fashion district. Ginger was very pleased to be asked her opinion of a new design. It was a wonderful diversion from the serious investigative work that she and her former sister-in-law, Felicia Gold, often engaged in at Lady Gold Investigations.

The office of Lady Gold Investigations was on Watson Street, just around the corner from her Regent Street shop, so the walk there was short, and her beloved Boston terrier, Boss, was quite eager to go for another stroll.

It was a sunny London day and the high windows of the shop ensured that plenty of light fell in, making the space bright and inviting. The white marble floors and the creamy walls, set off with intricate painted gold mouldings and electric crystal lamps, gave the shop a luxurious feel which was enhanced by the racks of designer dresses, gowns, and expensive accessories. It was well in keeping with the other fine shops found on Regent Street.

"Good afternoon," Ginger said as she entered. Miss Dorothy West, the floor clerk, was standing near the counter, about to make another sale.

"Good afternoon, Mrs. Reed!" Dorothy returned with a timid smile. Ginger was glad to see that the young woman had come out of her shell. In the beginning, Ginger had seriously wondered if Dorothy was going to be a good fit, and had feared she'd made a mistake in judgment by employing her. Dorothy's shy, nervous personality might have worked against her as she dealt with the high-society ladies of London who were not usually the forgiving type. However, after only the first few weeks, the young woman had grown in confidence. She particularly bloomed as she managed the upper floor with the factory-made frocks which attracted Bright Young Things with money to burn but little patience to wait for something original to be sewn up.

Ginger counted three ladies slowly wandering the ground floor at the moment, stopping to gaze at a particular designer gown or to feel the fabric of a dress by letting it slowly fall through their fingers. To Ginger, it was a satisfying sight.

She released Boss from his lead and commanded, "Go and lie down." The shop manager, Madame Yvette Roux, appeared just as the small dog poked his nose through the thick burgundy velvet curtain that separated the main floor from the back room and disappeared to where he had one of his little beds.

"Ah, Mrs. Reed," Madame Roux said. "So good that you and zee Boss could pop in. Zee day has been a very good one! And now you have come to see what our Emma is drawing, no?"

Ginger appreciated Madame Roux's experience as shop manager. The lady's sophistication and deep knowledge of modern fashions was a big asset to the shop. It had not taken much coaxing from Ginger to convince the middle-aged, widowed member of the haute couture to come out of retirement. When Madame Roux first heard about Feathers & Flair she had been only too eager to get back into the world of fine fashion.

"Yes, I am sure that once again it's something wonderful she has dreamed up," Ginger said. She joined Emma Miller behind the velvet curtain where the young woman sat in front of her large wooden drawing board, sipping tea and staring at a number of sketches. A rather intense person, she remained very focused on her art, but at the same time she was easy to work with, somehow having escaped the prickly attitude that so often plagued the more dedicated artistic temperament.

"Thank you for coming in, Mrs. Reed. I've been working on this particular piece for two days now and can't seem to decide on some of the final touches."

Ginger stood beside her and examined the drawings.

"Oh, this is quite clever, Emma. I do like those lines, and the shorter sleeves are rather daring."

"Hmm," Emma replied. "Let me sketch that in on some of these drawings and we'll see how it looks. Please give me a few moments."

"Certainly. I wanted a chance to check on some of the new frocks upstairs anyway." It was a few minutes after closing time and Dorothy was serving the last customer of the day. Ginger was about to make her way to the upper floor when she noticed Madame Roux staring at one of the mannequins. She had her left hand on her hip, and her right forefinger was idly tapping her chin, as if she was deep in thought.

Ginger nodded her head at the fashion dummy. "Planning on changing her suit for tomorrow?"

"No, I... erm, I don't know." She turned to Ginger with a look of puzzlement on her face. "Yesterday we received a beautiful fox stole and I was pleased with how it looked with zees particular dress and draped it over the shoulders."

"A Florrie Westwood design," Ginger remarked. The stole in question was by a very talented London dress designer who was also known for her beautiful fashion illustrations.

"Yes," Madame Roux replied. "Miss Westwood likes to use decorations like fur collars on her outfits so I added the stole to zees one." She gestured towards the fashion dummy. "Zee stole gave zee whole costume a certain *je ne sais quoi* so I told Dorothy to sell zee stole as a complete ensemble with zee dress. That is to say... not sold separately. I only put it on display just zis morning."

"Someone must have insisted," offered Ginger.

"Perhaps," Madame Roux said, one of her painted eyebrows arching. "But I am very curious to see who zis customer was. Please excuse me."

Madame Roux turned to seek out Dorothy, and Ginger went upstairs. She followed the latest trends in fashion religiously. Seeing the frocks in a catalogue was one thing, but to feel them with your own hands was another. Besides, who knew when a dress might come in that she might want to claim for her own collection?

A little while later she returned to the main floor intending to fetch Boss and leave for home. Madame Roux and Dorothy West were both standing beside the large oak desk that held the shop's ornate cash register. They were staring at the day's receipts which were spread out on top of the desk. Both women looked up at Ginger as she came down the stairs.

"*Mon dieu!*" exclaimed Madame Roux as she gestured towards the receipts. "We have been robbed."

CHAPTER TWO

"*O*h mercy!" Ginger said. "Are you sure?"

Dorothy's face flushed crimson. "We have gone over the receipts and stock several times now. There is no doubt about it. I am so sorry, Mrs. Reed. I really don't know how this happened."

Madame Roux concurred. "Highly unusual for a shop like zees."

"The fox stole," Ginger said simply.

"I have made a cursory check of zee shop," Madame Roux began, "The stole is zee only thing I can find zat is not accounted for. I have also asked Emma before she left to go home a few minutes ago. She has not seen it. "

"Should we call the police?" Dorothy asked.

"Yes, Dorothy," Ginger said. "Please ring them. Perhaps they can find something that we won't."

Dorothy nodded, and picked up the receiver of the elegant cradle telephone.

"But before you talk to them," Ginger added, "can you please tell me if Lady Isla Lyons was in today?"

Both Dorothy and Madame Roux shook their heads. All

four ladies who worked at Feathers & Flair had had experience with Lady Lyons and were very aware of her whenever she entered the shop. It was well known to the staff that the poor lady had a case of the "stealing madness". The items she took were always returned the next morning with an apology from Lord Lyons. No harm was ever done to any of the garments and the ladies at Feathers & Flair were instructed to turn a blind eye when they saw Lady Lyons leaving the shop with an unpaid item, whether she was wearing it or had it folded in her handbag.

"She was not in at all today or yesterday," Dorothy said.

"That saves me an uncomfortable call," Ginger let out a sigh. "In the meantime, let's put our heads together and see if we can come up with some clues."

Madame Roux and Ginger returned to the fashion dummy which had previously displayed the fox stole and stared at it thoughtfully. Whoever had stolen the eye-catching wrap must have surreptitiously stuffed it into a handbag. After a moment, they were joined by Dorothy.

"Do either of you remember anyone showing an interest in this outfit?" Ginger asked.

"No, no one asked me to remove this frock from the display today," Dorothy said. It was shop policy that should a customer want to try on an outfit in the shop, one of the staff would assist them.

"Nor me," Madame Roux added.

"Well then," Ginger said, "we know that whoever took it was very bold, and risked being seen in the act. What do either of you know about this specific stole?"

"It was ordered from a supplier called Berwick Furriers," Dorothy said. "The stole itself is a large adult fox. It has brown silk underlining to complement the fox's bright red fur, and features real glass eyes in the head. It has a gold clasp under the chin which attaches to a gold rope chain near the tail. The clasp has a little brass tag on it that says 'Berwick-upon-Tweed' which I believe is in Northumberland."

"So, one would need a rather large handbag to get this stole into," Ginger said.

Madame Roux agreed. "Oh yes. Zee handbag must be not only large, but also quite empty to accommodate the size."

"Did you recognise all of the customers today?" Ginger asked. "Or were there new faces?"

"It was a busy day," Dorothy said, "but I would say that I had seen most of those customers before. There were only a few that I didn't recognise at all, and of those, none were carrying overly large handbags, to my memory."

"Do you remember anyone with a large handbag who stopped at the cash register to pay for something smaller, like a scarf or something?" Ginger asked, "They could have fitted that in with the stole."

Dorothy replied, "Actually, there were no scarves sold today or anything of that size."

"Aha!" said Madame Roux as if suddenly getting a revelation. Ginger and Dorothy looked at her in surprise. "I sink all we have to do is try to remember zee ones that left without stopping at zee cash register and also had a very large handbag!" She clasped her hands together in front of her face in excitement at the brilliance of this idea.

Ginger and Dorothy shared a knowing smirk.

"Brilliant thinking," Ginger said, barely suppressing a chuckle.

CHAPTER THREE

*I*t was just after nine o'clock the next morning when Inspector Sanders from the Metropolitan Police stepped into the shop and took off his hat. The shop was empty of customers and the ladies were busy going about the process of beginning their day, but at the inspector's arrival, they gathered in the back room to be interviewed by him. The middle-aged inspector was one of the Metropolitan Police's more portly officers. He was dressed in plain clothes, with high-waisted, wide-legged trousers, and a narrow jacket that seemed in stark contrast to the body it was meant to cover, stretching over his stout frame, whilst his belt seemed to have one extra hole punched into it at the very end of its length to accommodate the girth of the man. His black shoes were shined to perfection, as was his police wallet badge which he made a point of showing to the ladies by holding it up to each of them for a moment longer than one might have thought necessary. He had thick, greying hair topped with a brown trilby which he removed upon stepping through the door, and a huge grey moustache that all but covered most of his mouth. When he spoke the thing wiggled and jumped like something alive. This caused Dorothy, Madame Roux, and Emma to suppress giggles whenever the man turned to speak to them. Combined with his merry, bright blue eyes, he brought to mind the American Santa Claus, rather than a distinguished member of the Met.

"Ladies, lucky for you that I'm just the man for this 'ere job," he said with some swagger. "I'm well acquainted with this kind o' perpetra'er, I am. You can rest assured you are as safe as fine ladies such as yourselves can be with me on the job."

He put away his notepad after taking down the pertinent details of the case. "This will likely become part o' the general ongoin' investigations into the series of shopliftin' we've 'ad 'ere in London in the last few months." He rocked back and forth on his heels while he clasped his hands behind his back. This caused his chest and stomach to extend outwards. Both Ginger and Dorothy involuntarily took a step backwards as if to escape any buttons that might suddenly pop off the inspector's waistcoat.

"You mean to say there have been other acts of thievery?" Ginger asked.

"Beggin' your pardon, madam, but we've 'ad complaints from shops of all kinds in the district 'ere. Seems like we might 'ave a sequential shoplifter prowlin' the streets of our fine city."

"Oh my!' gasped Madame Roux.

"Not to worry, madam," said the inspector as he turned to Madame Roux. "Me bein' a member of London's finest, I wouldn't let no one dangerous come near your fine shop. Besides, no one has been hurt nor accosted, so this perpetra'er ain't nothin' o' the violent kind it seems to me."

"So it hasn't been dress shops only that have been targeted?" Ginger asked.

"Dress shops, 'ats, shoes, anything to do with fineries and such. We got the best of the 'ole department workin' on it, includin' meself." He lifted himself up onto his toes, dropped back down, and cleared his throat. "We thought we 'ad the thief last week but it turned out to be the shop manager's nephew borrowin' a pair o' natty boots to impress his lady friend at a theatre performance. Now I'm not a married man meself, but if I was, I'm certain that Mrs. Sanders wouldn't appreciate me tryin' to impress her with a stolen article, if you know what I mean." He gave a wink.

"Oh my!" said Madame Roux again. Ginger glanced at her shop manager and had to look twice. Was Madame Roux fluttering her eyelashes?

"Oh yes, that one 'ad us busy for an 'ole afternoon. Anyway, not to worry, ladies. Ole Inspector Sanders is on the case. You can rest assured we'll find the culprit soon and 'opefully 'ave your fox back in the hunt so t' speak." He chuckled at his own witticism.

Ginger couldn't help but grin. "Have there been any robberies by this 'sequential shoplifter' that have occurred in our area?"

"Last week," Inspector Sanders said. "A couple of streets from 'ere a large leather 'andbag was stolen right off the display shelf. I don't know much about 'andbags and things but I'm told this one was an expensive one designed by some Italian bloke, I think. It was on special for 'alf price the day it was stolen. There was also a pair of women's leather gloves taken from another shop about a mile from 'ere and a straw 'at with fancy ribbons of some kind, as well."

"Goodness, the thief appears to have been very busy, and apparently has a wide palate for fashions," Ginger remarked.

"Apparently so," the inspector replied, "I think that's all for now. I thank you fine ladies for your 'elp."

Inspector Sanders donned his hat and stepped back out onto the street.

"What a fine man!" said Madame Roux after the door closed behind him. "It makes me feel good to know zere is such a brave young officer protecting our streets and places of employment." Ginger looked on in mild surprise while Madame Roux gazed out of the window to watch the decidedly middle-aged Inspector Sanders walk down the street, his lips pinched and his eyes bright as if he were whistling a merry tune. He was certainly not the type of man Ginger would have thought would catch Madame Roux's eye.

CHAPTER FOUR

*B*efore leaving the shop the night before, Madame Roux and Dorothy had come up with a list of three people that they could remember who fit the criteria of having not made a purchase, and who had come in carrying a large handbag. They had also sent a message to Emma to confirm that she had no additional names to add. As far as the three women could remember, there was no one that fit the criteria whose name they did not know.

Ginger had asked her employees to come in for a meeting before the shop opened.

"Even though I rang Inspector Sanders to let him know our suspicions," Ginger said, "I wanted to let you know that I'm of the mind to start my own investigation."

"I imagine you'll want to be your own client," Emma said.

"Precisely," Ginger replied, "Why not put Lady Gold Investigations to work? And, to be frank, I would rather catch this thief myself than have the police confront the person at some high society party or some such thing. It's not the kind of publicity I want for Feathers & Flair. I would much rather keep this quiet and discreet if we can."

Just then Felicia entered the shop. "Good morning, ladies," she said breezily. Ginger had asked her to come in to help with the investigation. Felicia had already proven quite adept at helping Ginger in previous cases, and one involving fashion would be just the thing for her.

"All right, let's see," Ginger said, pulling out her notepad as she slowly walked around the floor. "Our three prime suspects are regular customers here at the shop: Mrs. Penelope Carter, Lady June Hastings, and Miss Emily Maxwell. Now why does that last name sound slightly familiar to me?"

"Emily Maxwell?" said Felicia. "The actress?"

All four ladies turned to Felicia. She continued, "Why yes, I think I remember reading about her. She was in several successful musical theatre productions in the West End and in New York on Broadway years ago."

"I saw her film," Dorothy said. *The Wonderful Life of Mrs. Woods.*"

"I didn't know Miss Maxwell was an actress," Emma said. "She's come in for fittings on several occasions."

"What about our other two suspects?" Ginger said. "What do we know about Mrs. Penelope Carter?"

"She comes in quite often," Madame Roux said. "Zee lady eez in her mid-seventies if she eez a day. Her husband was a banker I believe, but he died a long time ago. She lives with her son and hees wife here in London. Last week she bought a dress right off zee rack and had a few alterations done. It was a leetle bit... eh, zee dress would have suited someone a beet younger perhaps."

"She has a huge handbag that she always comes in with too," said Dorothy. "It is hard to miss because of the bright floral design with the gold, purple, and peach details and the faux-tortoiseshell frame. A person could easily fit our stole in that bag, though it's hard to imagine Mrs. Carter doing that. She's such a nice lady." Emma and Madame Roux both nodded in agreement.

"And what about Lady Hastings?" asked Ginger.

"Also a widow," Emma said, "but younger than Mrs. Carter. She often talks of her husband and of their estate near Twickenham. He died in the war, a colonel I believe."

"Yes, she bought three dresses here when the shop first opened," Dorothy said. "She still comes in often, although she hasn't bought anything for quite a while now. She must have an assortment of large handbags and tapestry bags because she seems to always have something different. All of them are very fashionable and expensive looking. She had a leather bag when she was in yesterday."

"Thank you for your help, ladies," Ginger said. "Felicia and I will get to work on this. We will treat it as an official case for Lady Gold Investigation services. We will keep you informed."

"Will you simply confront the ladies?" Emma asked.

"Oh no, that would be rude and far too direct," Ginger said. "There are other ways of learning the truth."

"How do you plan on convincing these ladies to agree to be interviewed?" Madame Roux asked. "They 'ave no idea there eez a crime that 'as taken place."

"I have an idea about that," Ginger said. "We'll make it so each of these three ladies will be only too willing to have a visit from the owner of their favourite dress shop."

CHAPTER FIVE

*M*iss Emily Maxwell lived in a classy area of London which was characterised by the recent trend of the rich, mostly those without children, of selling their country estates to move closer to the city. This enabled them to live in the more manageable space of a flat, allowing them to reduce the number of servants they needed while still keeping up the lifestyle that was expected of their class.

"I'm very excited about meeting her," Felicia said as they crossed the ornately decorated lobby of the block of flats and entered the lift to the fourth floor. "And to think she's been in our shop numerous times and I haven't recognised her."

As the lift started going up, Boss let out a soft "woof" and for a moment struggled to maintain his balance on the floor. He was not especially fond of lifts.

"Sorry, Bossy," Ginger said. "I should have carried you." The lift was too narrow with the three of them plus the lift operator for her to bend down. Boss wagged his stump of a tail as the bell went off indicating they had reached their destination.

Miss Maxwell opened the door with a slight flourish. "Why hello," she said with a broad toothy smile. "What an honour this is to have Lady Gold come to visit me in my humble dwelling, and you too, Miss Gold." The aging actress was dressed in a stylish pink and grey waistless frock with a two-tiered, fringed hem. Even though she looked to be in her early fifties, she was still an attractive and elegant lady. She carried herself well and had a presence about her that was unmistakable.

The film star reached down to scratch Boss' ears. "Welcome to you too. Such a handsome fellow." She led them through a large hall and into a nicely decorated sitting room with a small fire burning in the fireplace, the coals just orange enough to drive out the afternoon chill. Tall windows overlooked the streets and afforded a very nice view of the surrounding area even though the day was a bit grey with rain clouds threatening. There was a pot of tea and a plate of chocolate biscuits on a small table. Ginger looked around for signs of a maid or some other member of staff but none was apparent at the moment.

"You have a beautiful home," Ginger said as they all sat down on the plush wing-backed chairs that were part of a matched set of furniture. Boss trotted over to the fireplace and lay down contentedly on the floor. Ginger noticed that the chairs and sofa were comfortable and of high quality but slightly worn in some places on the arms and backs, indicating either frequent usage or significant age, even if they were not noticeably out of style. There were two antique full-length mirrors in the room as well as a small standing screen for changing clothing, which Ginger thought was rather odd for a sitting room. Three dresses were draped over the screen as if someone had just tried them on. Ginger

LEE STRAUSS

thought of the shoplifting incidents in London that Inspector Sanders had alluded to.

"Yes. I've been living here now for almost a decade. I'm sure it pales in comparison to your Hartigan House, but I am quite happy here."

Miss Maxwell seemed to know a lot about Ginger, but she expected the lady spent a lot of time following the society pages, more than Ginger could claim doing.

"It is the staff's afternoon off," Miss Maxwell added, sounding rather apologetic. "Except for my maid."

"I must say, though I am not completely familiar with your work," Felicia said after a sip of tea, "I do have friends who are in theatre work in some way or another and they all speak highly of you."

"Why, thank you, Miss Gold. I am flattered." Miss Maxwell raised her hand to her chest and smiled.

"I've even heard you compared to Gladys Cooper, the famous film star," Felicia gushed. Ginger knew of Gladys Cooper. The beautiful young lady was a rising star in both film and theatre, and Ginger and Basil had attended a very successful play written by W. Somerset Maugham in which she had played the lead.

"Oh my word, now that is stretching it a bit," Miss Maxwell said with a laugh that Ginger thought was a bit forced and uncomfortable. "Gladys Cooper is young enough to be my daughter, though I suppose we do have some things in common." She cleared her throat. "Now then, tell me about this event at your fine shop. Feathers & Flair is one of my favourites, you know."

"As I mentioned to you in my note," Ginger said, "Feathers & Flair has had a wonderful opening year, and to celebrate we've decided to give away one of our ensembles to a loyal customer. What I haven't told you yet is that each of

64

the staff was asked to pick their top three favourites of our customers and put the names in a hat. Out of those names I picked at random the final three. Those three ladies will then be invited to our autumn celebration event where we will be unveiling our new models from Jeanne Lanvin, the famous French Haute Couture fashion designer. At the party, the final winner will be chosen and that person will be invited to choose any dress ensemble in the shop as a gift."

"Oh my, what fun!" Miss Maxwell said, clapping her hands together.

"So we wanted to personally visit each of the final three to extend the invitation," Ginger said.

"You mean I was chosen?" Miss Maxwell said, her eyes bright with anticipation. Ginger and Felicia both nodded and smiled.

"Oh my. What an honour! I must say you ladies have made my day today! And I love Miss Lanvin's designs. She has such a flair for evening dresses. One of my absolute favourites!"

"May I ask you a few questions, just to get a sense of why you frequent our shop?" Ginger asked. "I consider someone like you to be of very discerning taste and it would be valuable information to me to know what it is that keeps you coming back."

A little flattery often caused one to drop one's guard and be more open in conversation. Ginger had a sense that Miss Maxwell particularly thrived on accolade.

"Certainly!" Miss Maxwell said with obvious pleasure.

"How often do you come into our shop?" Ginger watched the actress intently as she sipped her tea.

"Oh, I try to come at least a few times a month."

"I am curious to know when the last time was." Ginger said.

"It was just the other day," Miss Maxwell said.

Ginger smiled encouragingly. "Were there any of our latest imports that caught your eye?"

"Let me see. I tend to love the bolder colours. Especially from designers like Paul Poiret, oh, and Elsa Schiaparelli from Italy. You have several Italian designs from her in your shop."

"Yes, she seems to be highly influenced by Coco Chanel," Ginger said. "How about our upper floor?"

"There were some designs there that I liked too, of course," Miss Maxwell said, "though I'm not keen on factory frocks. Forgive me, but they feel tawdry."

"It's quite all right," Ginger said. "It's not an option appreciated by all."

"We have one ensemble on display that seems to be of particular popularity even though Madame Roux just put it up a few days ago," Felicia said, jumping in. "I'm sure it will sell very quickly."

"Yes," Ginger said, "I wonder if perhaps you've seen it, Miss Maxwell? It's a Florrie Westwood ensemble on a fashion dummy display. We included a bright red fox stole as part of the ensemble."

"Hmm. No, I don't believe I noticed that one," Miss Maxwell said with a shake of her head. She reached out her hand and pulled the bell. "Would you ladies like more tea?"

A young woman wearing a maid's uniform entered the room. "Yes, Miss? Shall I bring more tea?"

Miss Maxwell looked at Ginger and Felicia questioningly.

Ginger smiled but shook her head. "We really should be going. We know how busy you must be."

"You may clear away then, Betsy," Miss Maxwell said to the maid.

The young woman looked familiar to Ginger. "You bear a

strong resemblance to a maid in my service at Hartigan House," she said. "Is your surname Weaver?"

"Oh my, what a coincidence," Betsy said. She curtsied. "You must be Mrs. Reed! My sister Lizzie has told me so much about you and about Hartigan House."

"I'm very pleased to meet you," Ginger said. "Lizzie has also mentioned you a few times to me. I'll be sure to tell her that I met you in person."

"Thank you, madam." Betsy smiled nervously, curtsied again, then left the room.

"I had no idea that Betsy had a sister," said Miss Maxwell, her eyebrows furrowed. "She's a serious girl. Pleasant enough, I suppose." Ginger noticed that she sounded a little disconcerted. Something about the exchange that had just happened did not sit well with the actress.

Ginger nodded to Felicia and they both rose to leave.

"Come along, Boss."

"Thank you so much for visiting," Miss Maxwell said. She accompanied them into the hall. "I am excited about your forthcoming event."

"One of the ladies from the shop will be in touch with you about the date of the party," Ginger said. "It will also be advertised in the papers so I am sure it will be well attended."

As they went down in the lift, Felicia said, "She seems like a very nice lady, wouldn't you say? Hardly a candidate for shoplifting."

"She's hiding something, I'm afraid," said Ginger simply.

CHAPTER SIX

"The next lady to interview is Mrs. Penelope Carter," Ginger said as she sat in Emma's chair in front of the sketching desk at Feathers & Flair. The shop had been busy all afternoon, and it was the first chance she had had to continue with the case. Looking at her staff as they gathered around her she asked, "Have we had any telephone calls or visits from our Inspector Sanders yet?"

"*Non*," Madame Roux said. "We have been waiting for heem to call me, I mean … us, but so far zere eez nothing."

"I rang Mrs. Carter," Felicia said, "and we can visit her anytime this afternoon. She's very excited about the dress giveaway."

"Jolly good." Ginger rose and headed for the velvet curtain. "We might as well get to it straightaway."

A soft tapping on the glass of the front door caught their attention. Boss looked up from his basket with a soft "woof".

"Oh, that could be zee inspector now!" Madame Roux said. She straightened her frock and adjusted her hair as she stepped through the thick curtain.

"Oh," Madame Roux said as she opened the door. "Mrs. Carter?"

Mrs. Penelope Carter smiled warmly as she walked into the shop. She was a petite lady with white hair, and had a joyful expression on her face. She wore a flowing yellow chiffon dress with a thick ribbon around the waist, and though lovely, the frock had gone out of fashion since the war. Her bright grey eyes twinkled as she took in the four surprised ladies standing before her.

"Can we help you with something?" Dorothy said. "We have actually closed for the day."

"Oh, so sorry," Mrs. Carter said. "Sometimes the time does get away from me. I was hoping to look for a new scarf today, or perhaps one of those cloche hats." Ginger and Felicia shared a look. The snug brimless hat was very popular among the flapper crowd but not the usual choice for ladies of Mrs. Carter's advanced age.

"I will attend Mrs. Carter today," Ginger said to her staff. "You can see to the counting of the receipts and cleaning up." The women all looked at one another questioningly but then dispersed to go about their duties.

"Now then, Mrs. Carter," Ginger began, "would you like to talk about the frock giveaway that Miss Gold rang you about, or would you like to shop first?"

"A frock giveaway? You mean to say you're *giving away* a frock? How exciting! Maybe I'll just pick out the frock now? Charles always likes it when I bring home something new to wear."

"I'm afraid the dress is to be given away at a special event we are having soon, Mrs. Carter. Your name is one of three that is to be considered. I'm certain Miss Gold explained this to you on the telephone earlier?"

"I don't really like the telephone contraption. Usually my

son George answers it or his wife, Mildred." Her smile was as sweet as a spring morning and her eyes twinkled like a little child's as she looked up at Ginger.

"So you didn't talk to Miss Gold at all?"

Mrs. Carter just nodded her head to indicate yes, but then she said, "I do like to talk on the telephone. I am sure if your daughter rang me we would have a wonderful chat."

Ginger felt a frisson of alarm. Mrs. Carter was making no sense at all.

"Miss Gold is actually my sister-in-law," Ginger said, "not my daughter." Besides, she and Felicia were only a mere nine and a half years apart. Ginger tried not to feel slighted.

Mrs. Carter furrowed her eyebrows in confusion.

"Did you say Charles likes it when you buy a new frock?" Ginger asked, hoping to keep Mrs. Carter's mind on track.

"Charles, yes, my husband. He's not exactly a fashion enthusiast, but he does appreciate a beautiful hat or an evening gown."

Ginger remembered that Mr. Carter was supposed to have died a long time ago.

"If I can't bring home a frock today," Mrs. Carter said, "maybe I can surprise him with a nice scarf."

Ginger allowed Mrs. Carter to browse the scarf rack whilst she moved to where Emma was standing by the cash register. "Can I please have the phone number for the home of Mrs. Carter?"

"Certainly."

Felicia joined the ladies. "Is there a problem?" she asked.

"No, not really a problem," Ginger replied, "but I think I had better ring her son. You didn't by any chance speak to him or his wife, Mildred, on the telephone earlier?"

"No, Mrs. Carter answered the phone," Felicia said. "I didn't speak to anyone else."

"I see." It was starting to make sense to Ginger now. She dialled the operator and asked to be put through to the number. Mr. George Carter answered.

"Oh, that's where she's got to," he said. "I am so sorry, Mrs. Reed. I know you are probably already closed for the day. We live only a few streets from your shop and she loves to stroll over there and browse your collections. She is... er, getting very forgetful these days and I don't know how much longer we can let her go out on her own. I want her to enjoy her life while she can."

"It's not a problem," Ginger said. "The ladies here know her well, and in fact they are quite fond of her."

Ginger had just completed the call when Mrs. Carter, sporting a new French scarf over her shoulder, walked breezily past the dumbfounded ladies standing at the cash register. "Thank you, ladies. Ta-ta." She gave them a little wave and another sweet smile and stepped out onto the street.

"Mrs. Carter," Emma shouted. "You forgot to..."

"It's all right," Ginger said. Emma and Felicia stared at her. Ginger dialled the Carter residence again.

"I'm afraid your mother's just walked out of the shop with a new scarf, Mr. Carter. It appears it must have slipped her mind to pay for the item."

"Oh no," Mr. Carter said. "I do apologise. Mother doesn't do things like that as a rule, only once before actually, at a milliner's shop down the street. However, since then I can assure you that our entire staff here have strict instructions to check receipts for any new item she brings home. I'll come into your shop first thing in the morning to pay for the scarf." He sighed into the telephone. "It does seem that she will have to be accompanied now whenever she goes out. This incident convinces me of that."

LEE STRAUSS

"By any chance did she come home yesterday with a large fox stole?"

"No, Mrs. Reed," Mr. Carter said. "We would've noticed something like that."

Ginger hung up the receiver and said, "That narrows it down for us a bit. Mr. Carter's quite certain Mrs. Penelope Carter didn't arrive home wearing a fox stole. One of us would've noticed if she'd walked out of the front door with it wrapped around her shoulders, anyway."

"The poor dear," Emma said.

"Yes, the family has some difficult times ahead of them, I'm afraid," Ginger said with empathy.

"That leaves Lady Hastings," Felicia said. "Shall we call on her next?"

CHAPTER SEVEN

$\mathcal{T}$he home of Lady Hastings was a small manor just outside Twickenham. Ginger, along with Boss and Felicia, drove through the stone gateway and up the short carriage drive to the grey stone building. Ginger guessed it had been built in the late Georgian era and had been added on to by a Victorian owner. Although it had certainly been updated since then, the whole place had a tired ambience, as if the current renovation needs, such as new paint on the window frames, were being ignored.

After instructing Boss to stay in the car, Ginger and Felicia were met at the door by an ancient man with a deeply lined face and wearing a butler's suit. He led them through a grand hall that featured a beautiful marble floor and a small chandelier. His movements seemed slow and painful and so it took a considerable amount of time for the trio to arrive at the door of a large, tastefully appointed sitting room.

Lady Hastings rose to meet them. "How do you do, Mrs. Reed."

"How do you do." Ginger motioned towards Felicia. "Of course, you know my sister-in-law, Miss Gold," she said.

"Yes, we have had a few conversations at the shop." Lady Hastings smiled at Felicia.

Lady Hastings looked to be in her mid-forties, although it was possible she was younger. Her eyes were fashionably made up with thinly plucked, arched eyebrows, dark eye shadow, and blackened lashes, but instead of adding a note of beautification, the makeup served to highlight the fact that her eyes were bloodshot. Ginger pretended not to notice the hint of sherry on the lady's breath.

Above the fireplace hung a large portrait of a distinguished-looking middle-aged man who was dressed in the uniform of a colonel in the British Army. Ginger gazed at the painting thoughtfully. Though the man was older than Ginger's late husband had been when he died, she immediately thought of Daniel, Lord Gold. How handsome he had looked in his uniform! A war widow herself, Ginger understood all too well the process of grieving and the toll it could take.

"He died in the First Battle of the Marne," Lady Hastings said.

"That was at the very beginning of the war. A terrible battle." Ginger said. "My husband was killed in Belgium near the end."

"I didn't know you were a war widow," Lady Hastings said. "But of course, that is why you are also known as Lady Gold."

"Yes, Lord Gold was Miss Gold's brother," Ginger said, nodding at her sister-in-law.

Lady Hastings looked at Felicia. "Oh, of course. I'm so sorry for your loss." The three ladies stared at the portrait, taking a minute of silence as if to pay homage to the fallen of the war and to those they had left behind. It was a small

THE CASE OF THE MISSING FOX STOLE

moment of shared remembrance and loss between the three ladies.

It could take a lifetime to escape the spectre of war, thought Ginger.

The ancient butler tottered in with a tea tray. Lady Hastings poured then said, "Now then, tell me more about this terrific event at Feathers & Flair."

After Ginger had given all the details of the party and the frock giveaway, Lady Hastings simply blinked at her and sipped her tea demurely. A far more restrained response then Miss Maxwell had given, Ginger thought. However, judging from the slight flush of colour that appeared on their hostess' cheeks and the upward tug of the corners of her mouth, she was equally excited about the opportunity.

Ginger watched Lady Hastings as she placed her teacup on its saucer with a noticeable shaking of her hands.

"When you set the date for the event," Lady Hastings started, "I would be glad to come, and I am happy that I've been chosen as one of the three finalists. I already have a large collection of ensembles as you can imagine, but your shop always has some surprising designs."

"If you don't mind, we would like to ask a few questions to find out more about why you like to patronise our shop," Ginger said. "It's a way for us to know what our customers prefer, and the answers may have a bearing on what we order in the future."

"Certainly. Delighted to be of help."

"Who are your favourite designers?" Felicia asked.

"I must include your Miss Miller on any list of designers," Lady Hastings said. "She really has got a flair for elegance and somehow carries that into even her more simple creations. I have bought two of her dresses. Then there are, of course, Coco Chanel and Jean Patou. Jean Patou in particular has his very own unique view of fashion that I find refreshing."

Ginger was pleased with her reference to Emma. "You are certainly familiar with the fashion trends of today, Lady Hastings," she said. Jean Patou was not really mainstream but was considered among the most daring and brilliant designers in Europe. Feathers & Flair carried several of his creations.

"When did you last buy a frock from us?" Felicia said. Although Ginger cringed inwardly at the boldness of the question, she carefully watched Lady Hastings for her reaction.

Lady Hastings shifted uncomfortably in her chair and said, "I don't know really, I guess it was a few months ago, I suppose. As I said, I already have a large collection."

Ginger noted the defensiveness in the words. There was also a slight quiver in the lady's voice and a slight dilation of her pupils, as if she was afraid of something.

"One has to show some restraint sometimes." Lady Hastings gave a wan smile as she said this, but it disappeared quickly and was replaced by a more pensive expression as if she was deep in thought for a moment.

"We have one particular display that Madame Roux is very proud of which features a large fox stole," Ginger said. "Did you see it?"

"I think so, yes. That is a more recent one, isn't it?"

"Yes, it is. What do you think of it?" Ginger asked.

Lady Hastings took a moment to sip her tea, as if she needed to answer this question carefully, then said, "I don't mean to offend, but I don't really like fur fashion. I know it's very popular, but it seems slightly uncivilised to me to be wearing an animal around your neck."

"Some have said so," offered Ginger. A very interesting

response, she thought. Is she being truthful or clever? Lady Hastings' facial expression was virtually unreadable but Ginger got the feeling that she wanted to say more about this subject and was holding back.

"Miss West and Madame Roux have both remarked on the beautiful handbag they noticed you carrying the other day," Ginger said. This time there was a definite look of panic that filled Lady Hastings' eyes, though just for a brief moment.

"Oh, that thing. It was a gift from an old friend. Nothing special but it does go with several of my suits. I carry it only very occasionally. It's just an ordinary handbag." She shook her head as if to say that this was a very unimportant topic.

"How interesting," Ginger said. "Would it be possible for us to see it? We're considering offering certain lines of handbags at Feathers & Flair and I'd like to get an idea of what a lady like yourself would choose."

Ginger knew this was being very forward, but she felt very strongly that Lady Hastings wasn't being completely truthful, and she wanted to get to the bottom of it.

"Oh, er, well. I suppose that would be all right." The look of reluctance in her eyes was unmistakable. She called out to the doorway from which they had entered. "Graves?"

After a moment the butler appeared in the doorway. "Yes, madam?"

"Could you please fetch my leather bag for me and hand it to Mrs. Reed? I think it's in the morning room." The butler bowed slightly and disappeared. He shuffled in a few minutes later carrying a large dark-brown leather handbag with a gold embossed frame and clasps. Ginger examined the exterior and noticed the name "Rafaelio" stamped underneath the bag. The word partially covered a discolouration defect in the leather.

"Very luxurious," Ginger said. "Do you mind if I take a glance inside?"

Lady Hastings nodded weakly in response. "Of course not. It is empty at the moment."

Ginger opened the bag but did not dip her hand into it at all for fear of seeming too nosy. The bag was completely empty with no tell-tale signs of red fur, though it was definitely large enough to hide the stole in. "It seems very sturdy yet lightweight." Ginger quickly closed the bag and handed it to Lady Hastings. "Tuscany leather is always so soft and durable."

"Yes," Lady Hastings said, looking slightly bewildered.

Ginger stood up to leave. "I think we have taken up entirely too much of your time. I thank you, Lady Hastings. Someone from the shop will be in touch to inform you of the date."

"I look forward to that," Lady Hasting said.

"That was interesting," Felicia said as they climbed back into the Crossley. Boss stood up from where he had been fast asleep on the leather seat, yawning and stretching. "I think she was a bit nervous during parts of that interview."

"As with Miss Maxwell, all is not as it seems at first glance," Ginger said as she put the vehicle into gear. "That lady has some secrets."

"Why did you ask to see her handbag? Were you hoping that the stole was still inside it?"

"That would have been too easy. No, I was going on a hunch I have had since Inspector Sanders came to our shop. He happened to mention some items that were stolen recently. One was a large Italian leather bag."

Felicia's eyes widened. "But how would we even know it was the same bag? There are many different types of Italian leather bags, even ones that size."

"Inspector Sanders mentioned that the bag was stolen from a display case and that it was on sale for half price."

"I'm not sure I follow you."

"Shop owners will sometimes reduce the price of articles that have a small perceived defect on them. Something that the manufacturer either didn't think would be an issue or that went unnoticed by both maker and shop buyer." She looked over at Felicia. "Lady Hastings' Rafaelio bag has a defect on the bottom. It's time to call the police."

CHAPTER EIGHT

*G*inger pulled the Crossley directly in front of Feathers & Flair and braked to a sudden stop to park it. Felicia, even though she should have been used to Ginger's driving by now, still seemed a little bit shaken from the short trip; she had been clutching her hat to her head the entire way, probably for fear of it blowing out of the window. Boss, of course, had loved every minute of the trip, as usual.

As they climbed out of the car, Ginger noticed a taxicab driver arguing with a distraught young woman across the street. Upon looking closer, she recognised her as Lizzie's sister Betsy, Miss Maxwell's maid.

"Felicia, can you please take Boss inside with you, and ring the Metropolitan Police to let them know what we've discovered? It would be best to speak to Inspector Sanders if he is available. Perhaps, when they search Lady Hastings' home we will have our missing stole. I will be in in a moment."

She crossed the street to the taxicab and said, "Is there a problem?"

"Mrs. Reed!" Betsy's eyes were wet with tears.

"Beggin' your pardon, madam," the taxi driver said as he took off his hat. "No problem 'ere, only the young lady 'asn't got near enough money to pay 'er fare."

"It's so embarrassing," Betsy said. "I should've checked that Miss Maxwell had given me enough money to cover things."

"It happens," Ginger said gently. To the taxicab driver, she said, "I will pay her fare." Ginger retrieved enough coins to cover the fare, along with a tip, and handed them to the cabbie. "For your trouble."

"Oh thank you, Mrs Reed," Betsy said as the cab pulled away. She was drying her tears with her handkerchief. "I get so upset when these things happen. Miss Maxwell sends me on errands sometimes without enough money and I don't quite know what to do. She insists I take a taxi instead of the underground because she has little patience once she decides she wants something. She likes a certain brand of biscuit that this particular shop across from Feathers & Flair sells, and also their imported cheese. She has a charge account here and at various markets. She likes expensive brands but I'm afraid she hasn't the money to suit her tastes anymore."

"It's quite alright," Ginger said. "You must find a way to tell her that she must pay the taxicab driver *before* you take the taxi, and to make sure you have enough to get back with."

"It is getting more difficult to work for her..." Betsy stopped suddenly, as if remembering her place.

"Whatever do you mean?" Ginger asked. She was not interested in gossip but her heart went out to the young lady.

"It's nothing, madam."

"Please," Ginger insisted. "Perhaps I can help."

Betsy relented. "Most of the servants have been let go and so I end up having to do most of the work. And Miss

Maxwell is behaving more and more strangely as time goes on too. She spends so much time just standing in front of her mirrors trying on different ensembles over and over again. She has more mirrors than anyone should want to have." Her hand flew to her mouth. "I am sorry, I don't mean to speak ill of my mistress."

"I can assure you, this won't be spoken about any further by me." Ginger paused, a thought popping into her head.

"Have you by chance noticed Miss Maxwell wearing anything new lately? Perhaps some accessory that you haven't seen before?"

A FEW DAYS LATER, the staff of Feathers & Flair were busy preparing for the frock giveaway. Though the promotion had originally been conceived as a ruse to sniff out the thief, Ginger recognised it as a good marketing opportunity and had decided to go ahead with it.

Ginger and Boss arrived just at the close of the business day, with Ginger carrying a large bag. She called everyone to the back room, opened the bag, and with a certain amount of flourish, pulled out a fabulously red, silky fox stole.

"I will let Madame Roux do the honours of placing it back on the fashion dummy." Everyone applauded politely and smiled as Madame Roux accepted the stole from Ginger.

"I have just returned from the offices of the Metropolitan Police where I spoke directly with our friend Inspector Sanders," Ginger said. "He asked me to thank you all for your co-operation and help in solving both their case and ours, which, as it turns out, were two separate cases after all."

"Is Lady Hastings in jail?" Dorothy asked.

"Yes, they arrested her soon after Felicia rang them. The

bag was conclusively identified as the stolen article. It turns out that Lady Hastings has had quite an appetite for expensive and exotic apparel, but no inclination to pay for it. For some people, even though they can afford to buy the articles, the excitement of actually stealing something and getting away with it can become an addiction. I fear in Lady Hastings' case this was further exacerbated by her propensity for excessive alcohol. Members of her staff reported her coming home frequently with articles of clothing of surprising variety.

"Of course they had no idea the items were all stolen, since Lady Hastings has always been an avid shopper. The police found numerous articles that had been reported missing, including a very large tapestry bag which must have been used to stuff the Rafaelio into. Quite a daring theft when you think about it. I think the alcohol was making her bolder."

"How sad," Felicia said.

Ginger nodded in sympathy. "Yes, I feel sorry for her too. She's a lonely lady who still grieves the loss of a good husband. Unfortunately she has turned to alcohol with disastrous result. The stealing madness probably started a while ago and worsened over time with the help of a lot of sherry."

"And Miss Maxwell?" Emma asked.

"I decided not to press charges against Miss Maxwell. I paid her an unexpected visit this morning with the purpose of claiming the stole. When she answered the door I simply asked her to return the stole. She was surprised, aghast, and repentant almost all at the same time. To her credit, she didn't attempt to deny it, but was quite adamant that it was her first—and last—offence.

"I told her that I had pressed Betsy for the information

and that it was not the maid's fault that I'd found her out. I also made her promise that if she returned the stole at once and did not force any repercussions on Betsy, I would not press charges nor make the incident public."

"Why did you not want to press charges?" Emma asked.

Ginger let out a long breath. "I know I sound altruistic in wanting to spare the famous film star her reputation, but the truth is, I'm equally concerned about the reputation of this shop. I didn't want it—or us—getting bad publicity."

"Did she say why she did it?" Dorothy asked.

"The motive is hard to pinpoint exactly, but I know she is a lady whose days of fame are behind her. For some people, the fading of the applause is more cruel than the fading of the money that goes along with it. It's as if you are trying to keep your slowly vanishing fame a secret somehow and so you keep your private life ever more hidden.

"For example, at our interview, when I realised Betsy was Lizzie's sister, it was clear to me that Miss Maxwell became agitated, though she hid it well. She was uncomfortable with any close connection I might have to her private life. In any case, I think the stole represented something new, exotic, and flamboyant, as a reminder of a time in her life when she was constantly in the spotlight. When she saw it on display here she simply couldn't help herself, and yet she knew she could not afford it."

"But will she do it again?" Madame Roux said.

"That's unknown, of course. However, even though I did not bring charges against her, I did tell Inspector Sanders about it all," Ginger said. "He promised to be discreet, but if anything else is reported missing in the future you can be sure he will be checking up on Miss Maxwell first."

"Speaking of zee handsome inspector," Madame Roux

said, "I must bid you all adieu." Everyone looked at her in surprise.

"Whatever do you mean?" Dorothy asked

"Zee inspector has offered to take me to zee cinema tonight. We are going to see *Zee Phantom of zee Opera*."

The four ladies just stared at her in astonishment. "I 'ave heard zees is a very frightening film so I intend to be truly 'orrified. Zee inspector will 'ave no choice but to comfort me." She paused. "Why are you looking at me in zees way?"

After a moment of speechlessness, Ginger and the other three ladies broke out in laughter.

WANT MORE GINGER GOLD?

Get Lady Gold Investigates Volume 2 - *The Case of the Recipe Robbery* and *The Case of the Museum Heist.*

MURDER ON EATON SQUARE
The Ginger Gold Mysteries Book # 10

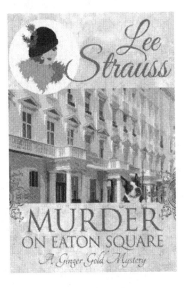

Murder's Bad Karma...

Life couldn't be better on Eaton Square Gardens where the most prestigious families lived, until one of their own dies and it's *murder*.

Ginger and Basil are on the case, but it's not a simple glass of bubbly fizz. The more the clues present themselves, the trickier the puzzle gets, and Ginger feels she's on a wild goose chase.

But as someone close to the victim so aptly quips, "One shouldn't commit murder. It's bad karma."

Reaping what one sows is hardly a great cup of tea.

On Amazon!

Did you know that Ginger kept a Journal?

Sign up for Lee's newsletter at www.leestraussbooks.com to get access to this exclusive content. Find out about Ginger's Life before the SS *Rosa* and how she became the woman she has. This is a fluid document that will cover her romance with her late husband Daniel, her time serving in the British secret service during World War One, and beyond. Includes a recipe for Dark Dutch Chocolate Cake!

Read on to learn more!

Join GINGER GOLD'S BOOK CLUB

Discuss the books, ask questions, share your opinions. Fun giveaways! Join the Lee Strauss Readers' Group on Facebook for more info.

Love the fashions of the 1920s? Check out Ginger Gold's Pinterest Board!

Join my Facebook readers group for fun discussions and first-to-know exclusives! facebook.com/AuthorLeeStrauss

GINGER GOLD'S JOURNAL

Sign up for Lee's readers list and gain access to **Ginger Gold's private Journal.** Find out about Ginger's Life before the SS *Rosa* and how she became the woman she has. This is a fluid document that will cover her romance with her late husband Daniel, her time serving in the British secret service during World War One, and beyond. Includes a recipe for Dark Dutch Chocolate Cake!

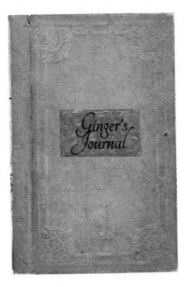

It begins: **July 31, 1912**

How fabulous that I found this Journal today, hidden in the bottom of my wardrobe. Good old Pippins, our English butler in London, gave it to me as a parting gift when Father whisked me away on our American adventure so he could marry Sally. Pips said it was for me to record my new adventures. I'm ashamed I never even penned one word before today. I think I was just too sad.

This old leather-bound journal takes me back to that emotional time. I had shed enough tears to fill the ocean and I remember telling Father dramatically that I was certain to cause flooding to match God's. At eight years old I was well-trained in my biblical studies, though, in retro-spect, I would say that I had probably bordered on heresy with my little tantrum.

The first week of my "adventure" was spent with a tummy ache and a number of embarrassing sessions that involved a bucket and Father holding back my long hair so I wouldn't soil it with vomit.

I certainly felt that I was being punished for some reason. Hartigan House—though large and sometimes lonely—was my home and Pips was my good friend. He often helped me to pass the time with games of I Spy and Xs and Os.

"Very good, Little Miss," he'd say with a twinkle in his blue eyes when I won, which I did often. I suspect now that our good butler wasn't beyond letting me win even when unmerited.

Father had got it into his silly head that I needed a mother, but I think the truth was he wanted a wife. Sally, a woman half my father's age, turned out to be a sufficient wife in the end, but I could never claim her as a mother.

Well, Pips, I'm sure you'd be happy to know that things turned out all right here in America.

Subscribe to read more!

·

ABOUT THE AUTHORS

Lee Strauss is the bestselling author of The Ginger Gold Mysteries series, The Higgins & Hawke Mystery series (cozy historical mysteries), A Nursery Rhyme Mystery series (mystery suspense), The Perception series (young adult dystopian), The Light & Love series (sweet romance), and young adult historical fiction with over a million books read. She has titles published in German, Spanish and Korean, and a growing audio library. She also writes younger YA fantasy as Elle Lee Strauss.

Norm Strauss is a singer-songwriter and performing artist who's seen the stage of The Voice of Germany. Short story writing is a new passion he shares with his wife Lee Strauss.

For more info on books by Lee Strauss and her social media links, visit leestraussbooks.com. To make sure you don't miss the next new release, be sure to sign up for her readers' list!

Did you know you can follow your favourite authors on Bookbub? If you subscribe to Bookbub — (and if you don't, why don't you? - They'll send you daily emails alerting you to sales and new releases on just the kind of books you like to read!) — follow me to make sure you don't miss the next Ginger Gold Mystery!

www.leestraussbooks.com
leestraussbooks@gmail.com

BOOKS BY LEE STRAUSS

On AMAZON

Ginger Gold Mysteries (cozy 1920s historical)

Cozy. Charming. Filled with Bright Young Things. This Jazz Age murder mystery will entertain and delight you with its 1920s flair and pizzazz!

Murder on the SS *Rosa*

Murder at Hartigan House

Murder at Bray Manor

Murder at Feathers & Flair

Murder at the Mortuary

Murder at Kensington Gardens

Murder at St. Georges Church

Murder Aboard the Flying Scotsman

Murder at the Boat Club

Murder on Eaton Square

Murder by Plum Pudding

Lady Gold Investigates (Ginger Gold companion short stories)

Volume 1

Volume 2

Higgins & Hawke Mysteries (cozy 1930s historical)

The 1930s meets Rizzoli & Isles in this friendship depression era cozy mystery series.

Death at the Tavern

Death on the Tower

A Nursery Rhyme Mystery (mystery/sci fi)

Marlow finds himself teamed up with intelligent and savvy Sage Farrell, a girl so far out of his league he feels blinded in her presence - literally - damned glasses! Together they work to find the identity of @gingerbreadman. Can they stop the killer before he strikes again?

Gingerbread Man

Life Is but a Dream

Hickory Dickory Dock

Twinkle Little Star

The Perception Trilogy (YA dystopian mystery)

Zoe Vanderveen is a GAP—a genetically altered person. She lives in the security of a walled city on prime water-front property along side other equally beautiful people with extended life spans. Her brother Liam is missing. Noah Brody, a boy on the outside, is the only one who can help ~ but can she trust him?

Perception

Volition

Contrition

Light & Love (sweet romance)

Set in the dazzling charm of Europe, follow Katja, Gabriella, Eva, Anna and Belle as they find strength, hope and love.

Sing me a Love Song

Your Love is Sweet

In Light of Us

Lying in Starlight

Playing with Matches (WW2 history/romance)

A sobering but hopeful journey about how one young Germany boy copes with the war and propaganda. Based on true events.

As Elle Lee Strauss

The Clockwise Collection (YA time travel romance)

Casey Donovan has issues: hair, height and uncontrollable trips to the 19th century! And now this ~ she's accidentally taken Nate Mackenzie, the cutest boy in the school, back in time. Awkward.

Clockwise

Clockwiser

Like Clockwork

Counter Clockwise

Clockwork Crazy

<u>Standalones</u>

Seaweed

Love, Tink

.